Kate's Lesbian Awakening

A Model's Erotic Adventures Parts 1-3

Bill Nichols

ISBN: 9798628740767

CONTENTS

1   Kate's Lesbian Seduction   1

2   Kate's Lesbian Training   Pg #

3   Kate's Lesbian Lovers   Pg #

1 Kate's Lesbian Seduction

My name is Katelin, but everyone calls me Kate. While I was in college, I found myself a little short of cash towards the end of my junior year. I had done a couple of photo shoots with a photographer friend back home and didn't mind taking off my clothes in front of a camera. In fact there was a dirty little part of me that thought it was kind of fun being naked in front of a man who is constantly giving you orders to turn this way or spread your legs open. So when I saw an ad posted online by a photographer looking for erotic models, I figured I'd give it a try.

I phoned the photographer to find out a little more. He asked me some questions as to where I had worked and what I had done and seemed satisfied with my answers. He told me that it would be a series of photos for a website, maybe a hundred shots and I was to be in a pretend lesbian love scene with another model.

I was a little nervous about working with another model for a lesbian scene, even if it was just 'pretend'. However, my nervousness lost out to my wallet when he told me the job paid $500! He gave me the address of his studio and asked me to be there by noon the next day for a test shot or two and if he liked what he saw, then we'd do a shoot at two tomorrow also.

Kate's Lesbian Awakening

I still wasn't 100% sure about doing this kind of shoot. I mean what kind of website was this? Also, my photographer friend had never asked me to sign a release. Then again, he also never paid me no $500 for a couple of hours work either.

I was pleased. The timing fit right into my schedule. The next day was a Saturday, I had some errands to run that morning, but knew I would be done by 11. That was time enough to get back to my place, change into something more appropriate and then head to the studio. It might be a little tight because I had to take the bus and the studio was on the other side of town. I wanted the job and sure wanted the money. I hoped he liked my looks. My boyfriend did, but he was on the school track team and they were out of town for the weekend for a meet. So, I was on my own. That was ok though, his birthday was coming up and I was going to use part of the money from this shoot to get him something special.

The studio was in a nice district, lots of little shops on a tree lined narrow street. I had some trouble finding the place but did. It was in a walk up above a baby clothes store. The photographer "Mike" was a nice guy, he had me do a turn around and show him my ID. He even said Please when he asked me to show him my breasts. I was determined to act as cool about it as him and pretended to myself, that he was a Doctor, so I wouldn't blush.

He liked what he saw and asked me if I could bring a set of high heels and some hose to the shoot. I had to tell him I didn't have a car and couldn't leave and be back by two.

He reached in his pocket and said, "Here's a hundred in advance make sure you come back! There lots of shops on the block."

So I shopped for the two hours and found the cutest little pair of black high heel high platform pumps They were all little straps and the shoes made my size six and a half foot, look like size four. I also bought the most glorious pair of black French nylons you ever saw. They were stay-ups and had a top band of beautiful intricate lace at least six inches wide. I knew my boyfriend would love them and got hot just thinking about how much they would turn him on.

Kate's Lesbian Awakening

The other model was already in the little change room when I got back, and she was lovely. Amanda was her name and she was a tall well-stacked blonde and had one of those I'm a so cool, haughty look that I wish I had. I'm kind of like a friendly puppy and am about as cool as jiggling jelly. She was really nice though and asked me what kind of modeling work I had done before. I had to tell her that it was my first erotic shoot and that I needed the money for my boyfriend's surprise birthday present. She told me not to worry; she had done a lot of these kind of shoots, as the guys just loved her tits. She would help and walk me though.

Though I was a little taken aback by her forwardness, I appreciated how nice she was being! Her breasts were perfect, a thirty-eight at least and I didn't think they were enhanced. She saw me looking at them and looked puzzled. I got embarrassed and blushed. I told her that, I was sorry. I was looking cause she had such a nice set and I was trying to see if they were real.

She said "They are Honey check'em out for yourself."

"No, I believe you."

"Come on Honey don't be shy. We'll be doing a lot more that in a few minutes."

I figured what the hell, she was right and reached out and touched her breast softly.

"Not like that love, give them a good squeeze! You can't feel if a woman has implants unless you really move them around. Use both hands."

So I did! I put one hand on each of her tits and first gently squeezed but at her discussed look, really squeezed them and moved them around.

They were real all right. I went to stop but she said. "Tease my nipples Honey, makes em stand up for the camera and the guys really love that."

So I tweaked on her nipples until they were hard. I wasn't sure about this, but she was right. This was just getting ready for the shoot.

Mike hollered for us, so I had to stop and get ready fast.

Kate's Lesbian Awakening

Amanda loved my hose and shoes. She said she liked to go barefoot and the hell with what the photographer wanted. She wasn't standing around in heels for three hours. I had brought my terry robe and we went out in the studio. There was a bed there, in a fake bedroom. Amanda wore nothing and was natural as anything when the Mike's eye's checked her out.

He had me remove my robe but that wasn't too bad, Amanda just looked bored and I pretended the same. Mike then had me go back and get my blouse and shirt and put them on. He said that Amanda would be the dominant and I was to be the young girl being seduced. I didn't know what a dominant was. But being seduced sounded nice.

We did a bunch of shots beside the bed. Amanda had to stand behind and over me, looking down while she disrobed me. It was easy for her. She had six inches on my height. I closed my eyes as she slowly undressed me. Even the constant, hold it, that's good, down a bit, hold it, another hold it, from Mike. Didn't let me lose the erotic mental image of my being undressed by my boyfriend. I was kind of turned on by it.

Mike then had us get on the bed. I was naked now also. We were asked to hold each other and kiss. That was nice, it was cool in the studio and Amanda's skin was warm. Her nipples were still hard and mine went hard also, in her arms. Mike had us touch our tits together and pretend to kiss again. Amanda gave me a real kiss. I was surprised when her tongue entered my mouth, but she whispered, "Relax it's just posing."

So I did and kissed her back. Mike told us go into a sixty-nine position, Amanda on top and I was lost at that instruction, but Amanda took hold of my shoulders and placed me on my back. Then got up on top of me. I was looking right up into her bare hairless pussy. Mike told me to stick out my tongue and pretend to lick. Amanda lowered her pussy just over my mouth and Mike started to snap some more pictures when he cursed and said.

"Take a break girls I'm having some trouble with this camera. I'm going to have to switch out my memory cards, I'll be right back."

I was going to get up but Amanda said. "Don't bother Sugar.

Kate's Lesbian Awakening

He'll be back in a second and will spend a week trying to get us back in this same position. Just stay there."

I laid there with her pussy just a touch away from me and she must have got tired cause her pussy kept getting lower and lower until it was resting on my mouth. I figured she didn't know, so I just let it stay there and breathed though my nose. Her pussy was wet though and I automatically licked my lips but touched her with my tongue. Amanda shuddered and raised up off me.

"Oh I'm sorry Honey. I guess I was getting a little too close." She said, her voice sounding a bit husky.

"That's Ok. I'm tied too. I was up at six this morning." I replied, still able to taste her womanly flavor on my lips. It had been a brief touch, but I felt myself stirring. What was wrong with me? I'm not into women... yet Amanda was beautiful and, I had to admit, I was turned on by having this lovely creature's sex right in my face.

I don't know what was taking Mike so long, but we just kept waiting. Soon Amanda was beginning to slowly lower herself back down and it wasn't long before her open pussy was back on my mouth.

I didn't want to say anything because she was being so nice, and in my innocence, I genuinely thought this was just her being tired. But there she was, her pussy resting on my mouth. Her womanly musk filling my nose with each breath. She was wet, and her juices were on my lips, tasted like strawberries.

I couldn't help myself; I was getting really turned on. I moved my head just a bit, trying to get more comfortable. When I did, my lips parted just a bit and I couldn't help but kiss her on her sex. Amanda moaned softly but didn't say anything.

I started to say something, or at least try to through a mouthful of Amanda's pussy, but Mike came back in and we started again. Mike said he liked the way it looked, my mouth right on Amanda's pussy, so she stayed there rather than lifting herself off me. He took more photos, some coming in to get close-ups of Amanda's face, some for close-ups of my face as I lay there. It was all dizzying me as I couldn't help but move my lips and occasionally brush my tongue against the other coed's sex. For her part Amanda moaned whenever she would shift herself on my face or whenever my lips kissed at her womanhood. I felt myself getting wetter and wetter even as I felt Amanda's juices moistening my own face with her heat.

Then, suddenly Mike was done with those shots. He took Amanda's hand and lifted her from me. I ran my hand across my face as I realized I was covered in her juices. Her flavor was on my lips and her scent filled my nostrils. I couldn't help but imagine what it would've been like to not just lay there, but to have actively tasted her, to have used my lips and tongue to please her. I felt a tingling in my belly at the thought.

Mike and Amanda had stepped away for a moment and he was talking to her quietly. I couldn't here what they were saying, but the auburn-haired beauty smiled wickedly and looked my way. She winked at me and stepped over to a table nearby. She was looking at whatever was on it, I couldn't see from my position on my back. I rose up, propping myself on my elbows and looked over just in time to see her turn back towards me. She was holding a long dildo in her hand.

I just starred at it. I had seen dildos before, even played with one by myself on occasion. This one was a little bigger than anything I'd ever used. It was molded to look just like a real cock, with ridges and veins on the surface, only it was a transparent blue and maybe 10 inches long.

Mike told Amanda to pretend to stick it in me and moved all around getting shots from all angles. As she moved around for the photos Amanda pressed the dildo's blue, bulbous head against my sex. I was already wet and the rubber toy easily spread my lips at her touch.

Amanda moved it up and down my slit and I couldn't help but moan as I felt it against my womanhood. Part of me wanted to grab her hand and guide the toy inside of me, it felt so deliciously dirty as this woman whom I'd met only an hour before expertly teased me. However, I was sure this was all just part of the shoot and that it was perfectly innocent.

Once when Amanda was shifting position, I moved my hips

slightly and then let out a little gasp of surprise and pleasure as the toy slipped into me about two inches. Amanda apologized, but didn't immediately pull the toy out, in fact she moved her wrist and it twisted inside me, the feeling sending a wave of pleasure through me even as she slowly pulled it out. I wanted to tell her to put it back, but I didn't, I tried to stay professional, like they were being.

Mike then had us do some shots where Amanda was standing up and I was kneeling at her feet with my tongue stuck out. He had Amanda move closer to me and again I found myself face to face with her sex. Only this time, my tongue was out and she moved herself so it was resting on the top of her slit, her clit right there, exposed and against me. I was just to pretend but then Mike announced his memory card was full and he stepped out of the studio to retrieve another.

I started to get up, but Amanda put her hands on my shoulders and when I looked up she was shaking her head no. So I stayed on my knees and didn't move.

Amanda took hold of my head in both hands and asked, "You ever been with a women before Honey?"

"No, I'm not a lesbian." I replied shyly.

"Neither am I Honey but you know some of the basics if you're going to do this work. You ever done a sixty-nine?"

"No."

"That's ok Honey. I'll show you the basics, it's just pretending. Lay back and stick out your tongue baby." She commanded.

I felt like I was in a dream as I did what this beautiful woman commanded.

"That's a girl, now if I were really a Les I would move my pussy onto your tongue like this." She said stepping around and kneeling to place my head directly between her knees as she settled down on me.

I started to move, but she gently squeezed her legs around me and admonished "No don't move now it's ok. Just let it sit there. Now I would just let my clitty move back and forth on your nose, just touching like that. See nothing to it eh! Then I would lower my hips like this and gently pull your mouth into my open pussy."

Kate's Lesbian Awakening

As she spoke, Amanda moved her body, doing what she described. I felt my breath catch in my throat. She was getting wetter still, her sex pressing down on my lips as she ground into me.

"That's ok Honey breath though your nose. Now you would just move your tongue in little licks inside me. Go on." She said in a husky voice.

I hesitated. Up until now everything was sort of innocent, at least in my mind. If I did what she asked now...

"It's OK we're not really doing anything, you're just going to taste me a little." She said as her hands reached down and began gently kneading my breasts. The moment she touched my nipples they ached, it was like she could read my body and tell what I liked as she took my nipples between her fingers and gently twisted them, just a bit. I couldn't help myself and I moaned loudly into her wet pussy, arching my back. This moved my face more into her wet womanhood.

Amanda groaned with pleasure as I writhed under her. "That's right, a little faster. Good girl. You're a really fast learner."

I was gently licking and sucking on Amanda's pussy lips, so intent on pleasing this woman I hardly knew that I didn't notice when Mike came back into the room. I don't know how long he'd been watching us before he cleared his throat loudly, startling me out of my sexual haze. I was embarrassed to be caught in the act of tasting my first pussy. I felt my face flush even as Amanda rose up on her knees lifting her lovely sex away from my lips.

"Sorry to interrupt something that I probably should've been filming." He said, a devilish grin on his face. "I just got a call and I'm afraid I'm going to have to cut this session short. I have to take care of some other business that just came up."

Amanda stood up and helped me to my feet. She gave Mike a bemused look. "Just when things were getting interesting." She said.

"Can't be helped ladies, I have to run." He said and stepped back into the little office of his studio.

Amanda shrugged and gave me a resigned, pouty, look. "Guess that's it for today sweetie. Still you are a natural." She commented as she stepped over to the side table where there were some bottles of water. She opened one and took a long drink. She handed it to me and I did the same. We were about to put on our robes and head to the changing room when Mike came back out. He handed us each a copy of the signed release forms we'd filled out.

"Keep these for your records, I've got the originals."

Then he counted out five one hundred dollar bills into my hand. He gave Amanda her money too and I noticed she got eight hundred to my five.

Mike was frowning. "Look I'm really not happy we had to cut this short. How about you both come back next Saturday and we finish the shoot? I'll pay you the same rate again."

I started to say no thanks, but Amanda nudged me before I could open my mouth and said. "That would be wonderful, I've loved working with Kate. She's such a natural." She said and gave me a wink.

Mike smiled "Great! We'll plan for the same time next Saturday then." He said, then his phone beeped and he pulled it out of his pocket. Whatever message he'd gotten I could tell he wasn't happy about it.

"Crap, I have to go right now. It's kind of a family emergency. Amanda, would you mind turning out the lights and locking the place up when you ladies are done getting ready to go? I've really got to leave now and I won't be able to make it back here today."

Amanda smiled broadly. "Of course sweetie. I'll take care of everything."

I slipped on my little robe and Amanda and I went off to the change room to dress. We were chatting away and I was bending over to get my things when Amanda suddenly let out a groan of pain. I turned around and she was sitting on the room's one chair, holding her upper thigh.

I asked what was wrong and she said she had a cramp in her thigh from the posing and asked could I massage it. I said sure and she motioned me to her.

"Just kneel down here Honey and massage this muscle in my leg."

Kate's Lesbian Awakening

I knelt between her legs and placed both hands on her as she directed and moved the muscle around. My boy friend gets leg cramps sometimes after a game, so I knew a bit what to do.

As I worked Amanda said, "Kate that little lesson of ours is what is causing this. Would you mind helping me to get rid of the cause?"

I didn't know what she meant but said, "I'm not what you mean…" I said nervously.

"Love it's all the tension that I've built up, you're so lovely and what you were doing with your mouth was just wonderful. I was hoping that you'd help me get some release for the tension that left in me." Amanda said and placed her hands on each side of my head.

She was gently massaging my scalp and her fingers played through my shoulder length hair. Her touch was exciting me and without even thinking I had turned more towards her. Now instead of both hands massaging her sore muscle on her leg, my fingers were moving lightly up and down her inner thighs. I'd never really been attracted to women, but Amanda was so beautiful and, honestly, the fact that my conservative upbringing made just thinking about being with another woman out to be a terrible sin…. Well that just made it all the more exciting.

As Amanda played with my hair and kneaded my scalp she was also slowly drawing me in closer to her sex. She was perched on the edge of the chair and her lovely pussy was right there. I could again smell her delightful, musky scent. I could almost taste that hint of strawberries that had been on my lips before when I was licking her. I was mesmerized, in a dream, as I brought my mouth closer to her waiting womanly lips.

"I know this is something new for you Kate, but it's like I told Mike, you're a natural." Amanda cooed as my tongue tentatively moved out and gently licked her labia.

Amanda moaned loudly as I slowly began moving my tongue up and down her womanhood. Her hands pulled me closer, pressing my face into her wet pussy. I wiggled my head and kissed and licked her with even more intensity. She squeezed my head between her thighs and moaned her approval of my efforts. So even though this was new for me, I guessed I was doing a pretty good job.

As I licked her, she reached over me and drew my robe down, off my shoulders. She couldn't reach all the way and stopped but my arms were tangled in my robe behind my back.

I started to try and free them but she said, "Don't worry about your hands Honey. You don't need them now. Concentrate on what you're doing!" she commanded and I obeyed, continuing to lick her up and down, probing inside her with my tongue as my lips kissed her flesh.

"Faster now. Oh that's a good girl. I'm gonna come real soon and my leg will be much better." She encouraged and I had a moments flash that I had started all this to relieve her leg cramp and now...

My musing was cut off as she griped me hard by my head and ground her open slit on my face, "Lick faster."

I licked her and she bucked her cunt on my face and nose. She had wrapped her legs around me at some point and her heels were pressing into my back as she climaxed.

Her body trembled as the wave of pleasure washed over her. I felt my own sex moisten and I reached one of my hands down to stroke my own damp, sensitive flesh as she quivered at the attention of my mouth.

She stopped shaking and I felt her relax, but she didn't release my head, so rather than stop, I stuck my tongue really deep into her and tasted her cream in my mouth. I felt dirty and shameful, a wanton slut licking this young woman's cunt. I loved it. She tasted so good. All the sensations, her moans, her soft skin, the taste, the smell, how beautiful she looked when I brought my eyes up to meet hers. All of my senses were stimulated by this erotic dream.

As she look down at me, sweat dripping from her as I worked her. I could see her bite her lower lip and suddenly she cried out "Oh God I'm cumming again!" and she began writhing about as another orgasm shook her body. She was beautiful as she came again.

After she came down from her second climax, Amanda parted her legs and gently guided me up from my place between her damp

Kate's Lesbian Awakening

thighs. I was on my knees, the robe still partly covering me as she guided me to her lips. We kissed and she sighed contentedly as her tongue ran along my lips tasting her juices from my mouth.

We kissed and her hands found the edge of the robe that still somewhat covered me. She skillfully worked it the rest of the way down my arms and it fell to the ground. I hardly noticed. Then she broke the kiss and began to stand, guiding me to my feet with her.

"We need to be more comfortable for this" she said and walked me out of the change room, her arm around my shoulders.

"On the bed Kate, you said you aren't a Lesbian so we'll do you, like you're used to." She said as she guided me to the soft matts we'd been shooting on earlier.

I wasn't sure what she meant, but my pussy was so wet, my stomach was tingling and all I wanted was for this woman to take me however she wanted. She put me on my knees with
my face into a one of the cushions Mike had laid around the matt.

Amanda moved around behind me, but told me not to look. "Just pretend I'm your boyfriend honey, keep your eyes closed and enjoy this."

I felt something hard probe at my pussy and I knew at once, it was the blue dildo we'd used before.

"Some guys talk dirty when they fuck Honey so I'm gonna pretend to."

She slid the dildo into my cunt until I could feel her hips touch my backside. I was so wet that it went in fairly easily, even though it was definitely bigger than any real cock I'd ever had. The hard fake penis made me groan with pleasure.

She started to fuck me.

Speaking down to me.

"Do you like this, you little bitch? Do you like me fucking you? Do you like it hard? Is this what you like?'

I tried to answer her, but all that escaped my lips was a loud moan of ecstasy as Amanda fucked me, faster and harder. My body jolted with the force of the slamming dick into me. I bit on the pillow, my eyes closed, it felt so fucking good.

She wiggled her hips as she fucked me and the dildo touched me everywhere inside. I cried out and almost came but she stopped and let me settle down. She never pulled the rubber cock out of me. She just stopped moving. I grunted and pressed back against her, starting to rock against it. I needed to get off!

"Stop moving, I'm the only one who can make you cum!" She commanded and I did as she said.

Finally, when I thought I was going to burst, she slowly began fucking me again.. She kept me like that fucking me and stopping, keeping me, just from my climax. My pussy was gushing and I wanted to cum so bad I started to beg her. But she wouldn't let me come. She kept up a stream of comments as she rammed into me.

I was lost in my pleasure and wasn't paying attention but thought I heard her say, "Oh I love this you little tramp, you little pussy sucker! You're going to eat my pussy again aren't you? You're my little whore."

I loved the dirty words she called me and I was just going to come.

When...

She stopped and withdrew the dick from me. I cried out on frustration.

"It's ok honey, we're gonna try something else now. OK?"

I was in a dazed state but nodded ok.

She shifted and she spit a thick stream of saliva right onto my asshole. Then I felt the tip of the dildo pressing against my ass, and stared to push it in.

I started to cry in protest but she said. "Quiet now, just relax, you have to learn how to take this also!" It hurt, but I didn't move, groaning as she pushed it into me, slowly one inch in, then she'd pull it almost out then push it back only a tiny bit deeper.

I felt my anus stretching around the long wide plastic prick. She fucked it slowly in and out of me. It felt, so different, at first it had hurt, but now it felt good. I felt so full! My pussy was aching with the need to come as she fucked my ass. I made me groan with pleasure. It was like being fucked in a second cunt I didn't know I had until now.

"See... I know what women like." She purred into my ear as she worked my body.

"I thought you would like this just relax your hole and let me fuck you now. That's a girl, just enjoy it."

She moved the dildo in and out of me faster and faster. As she screwed my asshole she reached down and played with me. Her fingers found my clit and she began to squeeze and kneed my little bud as she fucked my ass with the dildo.

That was it, I went over the edge and came harder than I ever had before. I was trembling, my knees shaking as the shudders of pleasure ran through my body.

"That's it Kate, cum for me. Cum for another woman." She whispered and leaned down to plant soft kisses on the skin of my back as my orgasm finally subsided.

She pulled out of me and let me rest a few moments. Then she moved up to snuggle against me. We kissed and teased each other. Time seemed to have no meaning, but eventually she pulled away from me. There was a devilish grin on her face.

"You know, I have a few friends who I think you should meet. I can't wait for the next photo shoot with Mike!"

Kate's Lesbian Awakening

Kate's Lesbian Awakening

2 Kate's Lesbian Training

I'm Kate and when I went for an erotic modeling session I knew it was going to be interesting… I didn't know it was going to be this exciting though! The photographer, Mike, was paying me $500 to pose nude and in simulated sexual positions with another model. The model's name was Amanda and she was so hot! I'm not normally attracted to women, but seeing her, I could understand why guys like women!

Like me, Amanda was a college Coed, though I still had a bit of time left in school and she was nearing graduation. Though the age difference was slight, the experience gap was huge. She clearly did this kind of thing all the time and quickly took me under her wing, or maybe I should say, between her legs, to show me the ropes.

While Mike was there the sexual situations had remained simulated… mostly. But Mike had to leave suddenly for an emergency and left us to lock up the studio. Amanda had complained about sore muscles and gotten me to give her a massage. That had quickly led to me helping her really release all her tension, through orgasms! I'm not gay, in fact, I'd never really considered being with another woman, but she was so beautiful and her words and touches so enticing… I couldn't resist.

Kate's Lesbian Awakening

I figured we were done after our first round of my oral affection, but I was wrong. Amanda made me lick her until she came again. She was kinda rough with me and my hair hurt where she had pulled it. But she told me what a good job I had done just like a real lesbian and that I was going to do just fine next week when we did another photoshoot. I was really proud and had to admit to myself that had enjoyed fooling around with her.

My boyfriend and I screw like normal people but he doesn't worry too much about me. Actually, that's an understatement, he usually has had too many beers to fool around much, if he isn't going to fall to sleep. Most often, he just gets me to undress and quickly screws me untill he comes. I don't usually get off myself and have to use my fingers after he leaves. His cum in me makes my pussy slippery and I come real fast, but at the same time, it's just not the same as having someone else take care of you.

After a long time touching and caressing each other, we finally got dressed. She told me that I should wear my new shoes to break them in and learn to walk in them properly. I told her, I didn't want to wear them on the bus. She said, she'd give me a lift home and when I said she didn't have to, told me not to be stupid as I was carrying quite a lot of money and it was getting dark.

I was surprised it was past six, time really does fly when you're having fun. I thought about it and finally decided she was right. I waited while Amanda made a couple of calls on her cell phone, We left the studio and went down to her little sports car. She was right I had to learn to walk in these heels! It wasn't the first time I'd worn high heels, but these were taller and the heel more pointed than anything I'd ever tried. I probably would have fallen during a long photo shoot, wearing them.

Amanda asked me all sorts of friendly questions about where was I from and did I live with my boyfriend and how did I meet him, stuff like that. Just casual conversation, but it did feel odd to me. I'd never just had sex with someone I didn't know before, so sharing mundane details of my life with her, after all we'd done together seemed… odd. Anyway, I told her about how I came from a really small town in the Bible belt and had left home last year for college. I had also left home to make it easier for my folks to get along, money was tight for them and I had a full academic scholarship, so it was easier on them with me in school. Plus, I was working on a degree, I hadn't chosen a major yet, but whatever it was, having a degree should help me get a job.

She asked me about my job at the restaurant too. It didn't pay hardly anything but I didn't need much money to live on because of the scholarship. I also told her how, I had meet my boyfriend while I was watching one of the school's track meets and seen him running. We had started dating almost immediately.

We didn't live together. I had, just a single room in the dorms and really wasn't supposed to have male visitors at night but that was ok. My boyfriend only came over once in a while. He had an apartment off campus and we usually 'played' there. Of course with track season in full swing, he was on the road a lot.

Amanda asked me if there were anymore at home like me but I told her no I was an only child. She smiled at that and patted my leg. I sat and enjoyed the car ride but I had to tell her finally that I thought we were going the wrong way? She laughed and said she was dying for a coffee and thought I'd like one too. So we were just going to stop of at her place for a while. I thought that was nice. I had learned to drink coffee at the restaurant but didn't like it too much it was so bitter but I did want to see her place.

I asked her about what she was studying at school and what she did for money and she told me mainly modeling and some other things from time to time. Her car was new and real nice so she was sure doing ok. I knew I couldn't afford one, even if I did manage get my driver's license.

She also explained to me that she 'cost shared' her place with two other girlfriends and they did some part-time modeling also. This explained to me how she could afford to live off campus and have a car. I had no concept of having money to burn so I was impressed.

Kate's Lesbian Awakening

Her apartment was in a ritzy building in a nice district of town. We didn't even have to park on the street. She pulled into a underground parking garage and we took an elevator up to her apartment. I was shocked by how nice everything was. I figured cost sharing meant it would be a small place, not a luxury apartment. Amanda seemed to have it all for a college student!

She let me go in first and her girlfriends were home. She introduced me to Stacy and Melony and then two other friends. Linda and Pam who were over visiting. I wasn't surprised when Amanda told me they were models because they all looked so pretty and were dressed so sexy.

This was especially true for Stacy, she was a knockout, about my height but had a tiny perfect body on her. I had to shake my head, before my 'simulated' sex with Amanda for our photo shoot, I'd never really looked at other women, now I felt like all I was doing was eyeing these sexy ladies.

Amanda made us coffees and her girlfriends asked us how the session had gone. Amanda told them the truth. How we had started the session but Mike had had an emergency and had to leave. She included the fact that we had been paid and some of the girls nodded in approval.

The girls made some jokes about what kind of emergency did she mean that would make a man leave a sexy photoshoot like that and they all laughed. We sat around in some soft leather couches and talked. The coffee Amanda gave me was nice but had a funny taste. I asked her what kind it was and she told me Irish coffee. Oh, that explained it. There was whiskey in the coffee. Still it was really good and I wasn't driving so I didn't care.

Amanda told them all how I was pretty new at modeling but was anxious to learn. They asked me what I had done before and I told them. Amanda made me another coffee and after I drank that one I had to go to the bathroom.

When I came out everyone was on the balcony smoking so I wandered out to join them. They were sharing a home rolled cigarette and passing it around. I don't smoke but relented to give it a try when they passed it to me. I took a puff but didn't recognize the flavor. I asked what kind of tobacco it was and Stacy said she wasn't sure, a friend made them up for her.

We chatted and looked out over the city at the pretty night and the cigarette was passed to me two or three times. Stacy had to tell me to hold in the smoke and not to waste it. I guess it cost money to have someone roll them for you and I did as she said. Breathing it in deeply and holding it in as long as I could, just like she told me. She was right, it seemed the smoke had more effect or something but the coffees were making me a little dizzy.

Amanda asked if I was ok and I said I was just tired or something. She told me too much coffee could have that effect and we went back inside. One of the girls put on some music and we sat around enjoying the music having a giggle fit at all the jokes being told.

Amanda told the gang how this had been my first real erotic shoot and that I'd never done simulated sex scenes with a man... or a woman. She then explained how she was helping me learn to do it properly.

We all laughed about this, but then Amanda talked Linda into getting up and doing some posing to show me how. Linda did a strip tease in slow motion for us and we were all laughing away. She pretended I was the camera and showed me all of her body real close up.

She even spread her ass cheeks and wiggled her bare bum right in my face. Then the girls got Pam to strip and she did a sexy dance for us and laid down on the floor in front of me. Spreading her pussy open with her fingers. The girls made a bunch of rude comments just like the guys would, but it was all in fun.

Stacy was next but, said that she wanted to undress with me also just like at a session. Melony said ok we'll do a pretend shoot and went and got a camera. Stacy had me stand up and Melony gave us instruction as to how to stand and told Stacy what to unbutton on me. As she did I noticed that Melony was also taking pictures. The flash going off made everything seem just like a real photoshoot, even if it didn't have the lights and such like Mike had used.

The girls were real serious as Stacy slowly removed all of my clothes except for my hose and heels. She, like Amanda, gave me a passionate kiss and as she did, out tongues met as we posed. Stacy kept her clothes on and just stripped me naked as Melony directed, like a real photographer.

Everything was so sexy and the girls were all so nice. I was really enjoying myself. Amanda gave me another coffee. I knew I was buzzing from the liquor in it and that's why I was feeling a little dizzy. I didn't care, the coffee tasted great and I was feeling really good. Being naked in front of the girls was also making me feel funny, a flutter in my tummy that was deliciously warm, like the first hint of an orgasm.

Stacy walked me over to each of the girls to show them my body. They all said I had nice skin and that I was very pretty and fresh looking. They had me do all sorts of poses for them, the camera keep flashing on me. Everyone ran their hands over my tits and my bum and then between my legs admiring my skin. As they touched my sex, I would feel a finger slip between my lips and as it did I would feel the moistness of my excitement.

They had all gotten dressed again and I was the center of attention being the only one naked. Amanda asked if anyone wanted to help me learn to do more explicit scenes. Everyone nicely offered but Stacy said she was going first.

She walked over and shooed everyone else off the couch and sat down on its edge and lay back. She was wearing a miniskirt and high heels but had on panty hose. I could see her panty crotch as her shirt rode high up on her hips. The other girls gently pushed me in front of her and stood around us.

"Ok Honey Let's get you going, take my pantyhose off me first." Stacy commanded.

I had to get down on my knees to reach under her skirt, she lifted her ass as I began to pull them down.

"Go slow for the camera Honey. Always do everything real

slow." She whispered to me.

I pulled them down her hips and she raised up to assist me. My hands drew her hose down her smooth shaved legs. The pantyhose were real tight on her and I had to use my hands to roll the nylon down her legs, one at a time. I was just taking them off one of her feet when Stacy stopped me.

"Honey, in some of the scenes we have to do a pretend Les foot thing. We'll work on that. Take em off the rest of the way, only just use your mouth."

I was confused but someone helped me by taking a hold of my head and pushed it gently until my lips were on Stacy's ankle.

"That's good Honey, now kiss my ankle and use your lips to take my hose off. No, take your time, lick it a bit. That's good now take the hose in your teeth and pull it off my foot. Stop now. Open up I'm going to put my toes in your mouth. Its ok we all do this, that's good, now nibble gently on my toes, good girl."

Melony was still taking pictures and the flash was going off like crazy. Stacy had me draw the hose completely off her feet using my lips.

"Now Honey lick my feet, here, do the bottoms, oh that tickles, No! Keep licking em. Here, suck on my toes now, that's good, you're going to be good at this. Lick between my toes, slowly, let Melony take some pictures, that's good, each toe now. That feels great. Are you having fun? I think you are, you do that so well, but we'll have to have you practice that a lot to make it look like real. Open up wide now, I'm going to put both my big toes in your mouth."

I felt like I was floating outside of myself as I did what this beautiful creature commanded. I didn't think, when she told me what to do, I did it. Stacy giggled as her toes slipped between my lips.

"Isn't this weird, we sometimes have to do this and only the most special models get to do things like this. It is nice that you take to it so well. Suck'em, that's right, get them nice and wet." Stacy purred as I worked my mouth in and around her toes, sucking and licking with abandon.

"Ok now let's try something else. Move back."

Kate's Lesbian Awakening

I wiggled backwards and she rolled over and slid down on her knees on the floor. She lay with her chest on the couch, her legs spread wide apart. She reached behind her and took hold of her ass cheeks, pulling them apart revealing her little puckered pink anus. She looked back and smiled at me.

"Now we'll teach you some anallingus. Would you like that?" She asked in a husky, sexy, voice.

I hesitated. I'd tasted Amanda's pussy, but this was something new and it felt dirty.

"Help her girls." Stacy commanded as I hesitated.

I wasn't sure what to do but the girls around us helped me again and hands gentled my body right up behind Stacy. A set of hands on my head firmly pushed my mouth down touching on Stacy's bum. I resisted, pushing back with my hands. My head was spinning, I wasn't sure I was ready for this.

Amanda was behind me and gently stroked my body, soothing me...

"What's the matter Honey, Oh I know what's wrong. Here, this will help, sometimes we have to do things we are not sure we like but it's all just pretend. We'll do some bondage. That'll makes you feel like you have to do it and don't have any choice. Give me your arm." Amanda ordered.

"No!" I said shaking my head.

Amanda made a 'tsk, tsk' sound and wagged her finger at me. "Sweety, you're not going to go very far as a model if you aren't willing to try new things. Don't fight me baby, it's just pretend. We all play that we're being made to do it and it's kind of fun."

Her voice was soothing and I was buzzed from the Irish coffee, so I nodded and let her have my hand.

"Now the other arm." She said and I moved my hand back to her and bound it to the other one behind me.

"Good. I'm gonna tie them behind you. See! Now you're not in control, just let Stacy tell you what to do. You're doing really great so far."

Kate's Lesbian Awakening

I was nervous, but at the same time I felt myself getting wet. My hands tied behind me, nude before these women I barely knew, it was so exciting.

"Ok, girls she's ready now, talk really dirty to her I think she likes that. Use your hands on her, stoke her body, get her warmed up. Pam's gonna take her, while she licks."

Hands once more pushed my head into Stacy's backside. I did feel better when I was tied and felt as if I was being made to do it. I just closed my eyes and did as Stacy directed.

"OK Honey just put your nose in my hole. That's right push it in. Good hold it there while Melony gets the shot. OK Now pretend to smell my asshole, harder I want to hear you. That's good, you do that good... Ok put your hot little tongue in there, go on do it. Pam help her, make her!"

I pushed my tongue out and tentatively licked Stacy's asshole. The young blonde shivered with pleasure as my tongue touched her in that most forbidden place.

I heard Pam's voice whisper in my ear, "Go on you little slut, lick Stacy's asshole,

Stick that tongue out further. Good! Now, lick her, that's right lick her all around her brown ring. Inside now, make your tongue hard... Melony, You getting this?"

Melony made a noise that I guess meant she was catching my degradation on camera. I wondered briefly if the photos would end up on the internet. Then another thought hit me, I opened my eyes and looked to my left. One of the other girls had her phone out and I was sure she was taking video. The thought that me, licking another woman's asshole might make it on the internet for anyone to see... Oh God, I was more aroused now than I think I'd ever been in my life.

I turned my full attention back to Stacy's delicious looking ass and pushed myself in farther.

Amanda must've liked that because she stoked my head and whispered. "Good OK now hold your tongue out and I want you to remember when you kissed your boyfriend last. Remember that passionate kiss? Now I want you to pretend Stacy's ass is your boyfriend and I want you to French kiss her!"

The instructions were so simple, yet so lewd. I did as she asked though. I thought of kissing someone, only it wasn't my boyfriend, it was Amanda who came to mind. I imagined my tongue sliding between her lips and twirling around her mouth.

As those thoughts filled my mind I pressed my tongue against her puckered little pink asshole. I curved it and pushed it into her."

"That's it" Amanda purred as Stacy moaned with pleasure.

"Now push in as deep as you can go and wiggle your tongue around, deeper, good! Taste her. Keep kissing her ass like it was your lover's mouth... or maybe my pussy." She said as she stroked my ass.

"That looks so nice! You're a natural at modeling and you're doing just fine! Isn't she girls?" Amanda said, letting her finger move down to my own upturned ass and pushing ever so lightly against my asshole.

I shuddered with pleasure as she touched me.

"Now just keep licking on that asshole while I have some fun, with you too!" Amanda cooed.

I felt her hand move away from my bum for a moment and then it was back only one of the other girls was helping her. The other girl pulled my cheeks apart as Amanda gently applied some slippery fluid on my rear hole. She stuck her finger right inside me and wiggled it around, lubricating my anus.

I started to rise up but the hands that had been parting my ass cheeks now moved to hold my head back on Stacy's ass.

"It's Ok Honey, You've done this before and you liked it. Its just practice." Amanda said and then I felt the hands leave my head and someone lightly touch me as they moved behind me.

"Now we're going to watch and Pam's put on this nice new strap on dildo and she's gonna fuck your ass and you'll love it. Just relax and open up that little hole. That's right, feel that big prick sliding into you."

I felt something push against my lubed asshole. It was definitely bigger than a finger. It pressed against me and I felt my asshole stretch to admit it. Oh my God! I'd never let anyone do me in the ass and now Pam was behind me with a strap on and she was sticking it my ass while the other girls watched... and photographed my first ass fucking!

At first it hurt, the stretching and the pressure on my ass, but after the head of the fake cock was in me I was surprised by how good it felt.

Amanda moved up next to me and stoked my head as she gently pushed my face deeper into Stacy's ass. "Doesn't that feel nice? Melony, move around here so you can get the shot. Go for it Pam, do her, she likes to be pounded really hard."

Pam did, she fucked the dildo into me like there was no tomorrow. The prick was bigger than the one Amanda had used on me and stretched me something awful. It hurt as she fucked my ass but it also felt so nice. I could hardly concentrate on licking Stacy while I was being fucked.

I was surprised to feel myself building to an orgasm. No one had touched my pussy since I started licking Stacy, but I was feeling the stirrings in me. The delicious warmth spreading from my pussy up into my belly. With each stroke of the dildo into my ass I felt myself drawing closer to cumming.

As my body tensed the girls around us were making all sorts of crude comments. Like "fuck that little pig" and "ream her ass good", but I wasn't listening. I just whimpered because it felt so pleasurable being screwed in the ass.

Then it hit me. Stacy was moaning from my tonging her asshole and between that and the comments and being fucked... it was all too much. My body shuddered and I came. It was so intense. I was on my knees, braced against Stacy's ass and that was good because my legs would've buckled under me if I'd been standing. I moaned into the blonde beauty's ass as I came and the women around me lewdly cheered as I shivered with pleasure.

I felt Pam pulling the dildo out of me. It came out of my violated ass with a wet, slurping pop. I felt weak form the abuse to my ass, but also from the intensity of my climax.

"Look at my little slut in training!" Amanda said proudly as she stroked my hair. "My little darling didn't even stop licking you're ass when she came Stacy, isn't she amazing?"

Without any time to recover, I felt hands pulling me up and Stacy moved around to lay down on the couch, on her back. My face was pulled into her open wet crotch and she guided my mouth around where she wanted me. She had me lick up and down her slit and then told me to suck her erect clit into my mouth and softly chew on it. She swirled her hips around on my face.

Stacy was groaning with pleasure as I licked her cunt. I moved my eyes and say Melony still taking pictures and yes, the other girl was still videoing me. Now instead of being fucked in the ass she was catching me eating pussy.

Stacy rose up and grabbed my hair pulling me down into her pussy.

"Faster! Harder! That's it!" she screamed and I felt her body shaking as she came. She'd been so wet as I licked her, but now she gushed womanly juices into my mouth as she came.

As she was coming on my face I felt someone's hands on my ass. I was still sensitive from cumming earlier, but I was so focused on Stacy that I didn't resist as I felt warm breath on my cunt. Someone moved in and began to lick my pussy from behind me as I was licking Stacy through her orgasm.

This was all too much. I'd never been able to come twice in a row, but the combination of all the sexy women around me, Stacy's moans of pleasure and now the tongue expertly teasing my womanhood... It was just too much and I shivered into another mind blowing orgasm.

I cried out and dropped flat on the floor as I felt a spasm of pleasure as Amanda, pulled me up, away from Stacy's dripping cunt.

Amanda's face was covered with my juices and she licked her lips. "You taste like a peach Kat. A yummy, yummy peach of a pussy."

She pulled me too my feet and kissed me. I could taste myself on her as we kissed. Then she pushed me back down on the couch next to Stacy. As I lay there on the couch exhausted I heard the girls around me talking.

"Ok, who wants her next?" Amanda asked.

"Here someone take this frigging camera while she does me, I want her mouth." Melony said.

"No I want to fuck her with the dildo!" Linda whined.

"Make her clean it, first she probably needs the practice sucking, before the guys arrive" Stacy said and I turned my head to look at her in surprise.

"The guys?" I asked and all the girls started laughing.

"Yes sweety, did you think this was just a ladies party? Don't worry though, they are going to love you!" Stacy said with a wicked grin.

This was going to be a long night....

Kate's Lesbian Awakening

3 Kate's Lesbian Lovers

My name is Kate, and I'm not a lesbian. I was raised to believe that kind of thing was a sin and I certainly have never been attracted to women... until now. It started when I went for a modeling job. I'm a college coed and needed some quick money. I'd done a few photo shoots before so when I answered an ad for an 'erotic' shoot I thought it wouldn't be a big deal. I don't mind the nudity, though I'd never done that before, so I figured it would be easy money. What I didn't know was that the shoot was simulated sexual acts. Even that wouldn't be too bad I supposed, except it wasn't with a guy. My partner was another college aged woman!

Her name was Amanda and though she was only a year or two older than me, she was an experienced erotic model. She helped me during the photo shoot and I was grateful. She's a beautiful woman with a figure to die for and a great personality. She set me at ease right away and worked with me to make the shoot look great.

The problem is that some of the shots got a little too intimate. Before I knew it I had my face in her pussy. It was so exciting for me, the idea of playing at sex for the camera, especially as the photographer's camera recorded us, I began really getting turned on. All the touching and being told what to do, it was exciting. The fact that I was raised to think it was a sin didn't make me shy away, instead it made me hornier and hornier as the shoot went on.

Kate's Lesbian Awakening

Accidental touches, licks and other intimacies, which seemed so innocent gave way to more after the photographer left us alone in the studio. I was a good girl and did just what Amanda told me as she instructed me how to make an erotic shoot with a woman look real. Yes… I ate her pussy. That wasn't all we did then either and I was shocked by how far I let her go with me.

Then we had to leave the studio. Amanda offered a ride, but rather than taking me home, we ended up at her place. She had an amazing apartment in the 'fancy' side of town. She explained that she could afford it because she had roommates. She lived with two other models, Stacy and Melony. When we got to her place there were two more models there, Pam and Linda.

It was practically a little party. In fact the coffee she served everyone was spiked with a healthy dose of whiskey and soon enough I was feeling really good and relaxed. So much so that when Amanda suggested that we all do a modeling shoot together, I didn't mind, they were all so nice. They were all so beautiful. It was like a dream as they had me take off my clothes…

They didn't stop there.

Soon enough Stacy was also naked. She had her ass up in the air and they wanted me to lick her asshole! I'd heard of doing a rim job. My boyfriend tried to get me to do that a few times but I wouldn't, it seemed gross. Now these lovely ladies were urging me on. I was hesitant so they helped me out by tying my hands behind my back. Being bound made me feel like I had no choice. I knew I could stop it at any time, but I didn't want to. I wanted to be made to lick Stacy's ass.

Soon my face was buried between her firm, round ass cheeks and my tongue was working her asshole like I was French kissing my boyfriend. It was so degrading for me, and yet I was so aroused by it. In fact when Amanda decided to taste my pussy while I was eating Stacy's ass. It was so hot that I came harder than I have ever cum before… then I came again!

When Stacy and I both had cum, all the girls began talking about what to do next. I was in a daze as they bantered back and forth about

Kate's Lesbian Awakening

whose pussy I was going to eat next or whose ass I'd lick or who got to fuck me with the dildo. All the while Melony had been taking pictures... and video. The thought that my sexy shame might end up on the internet, where anyone could find it, anyone could see me tasting another woman's ass... that was an even bigger turn on. But that part of me that was raised to think this kind of thing was wrong tried to assert itself.

"Amanda, we need to stop this, It's all a big mistake. I'm not really a lesbian!" I protested weakly.

Amanda looked at me and smiled that wicked, sexy, smile. "First off Kate don't worry about any guys showing up. I made sure no one called them." She said touching my arm in a reassuring way.

"However..." She continued "we can't just stop all this. After all, we're not all the way through this photo shoot. You want to be a real, successful, professional model right?" She asked.

I didn't say anything, but nodded my head in agreement.

"Good, good. That's the spirit. Now to do that you have to play along. Remember dear this is all just fun and games. It doesn't make you a lesbian to play with us. We're just doing a photo shoot and having a little fun that's all." She purred in a soothing voice.

"Melony, be a doll and untie Kate's wrists. The bondage thing is fun, but she needs to use her hands too." Amanda commanded.

Melony untied my wrists and set me up. Amanda then ordered the rest of the girls to clean up the place and, to my surprise they did. They put all the furniture we'd moved while shooting back and they even began getting dressed. Not Amanda though, she sat down behind me. She put her arms around me, cuddling me. I liked that.

When they were done fixing the room up, all the other girls stepped out leaving me alone with Amanda.

"How are you doing Hon? You Ok?" She asked.

"Yes... I'm a little tired. This has all been so... different."

"Honey. The girls and I got a little carried away with you. You're very pretty and to tell you the truth... very submissive. You made us all really horny, and it's a so much fun for us, educating you."

Kate's Lesbian Awakening

"I'm submissive?" I asked and as I did I realized the truth was it really turned me on to have them tell me what to do. I would do almost any nasty thing they wanted me to if they ordered me to do it. Things I would never do if they just asked.

Amanda leaned in and licked my earlobe then whispered "Oh yes Kate, you're very submissive. You don't mind that we are telling you what to do now do you?"

"No…" I whispered back.

"I think you quite like it don't you?" She continued, her hand moving from my shoulder to cup and squeeze my breast.

"Yes…" I said, leaning back against her as she fondled me.

"You know that we're using you for our pleasure as we teach you right?"

I whimpered as she pinched my nipple.

"Well, it doesn't make you a Lesbian to play with us, everyone is a little Bi, some more than others. You seem to like to be made to do things and to be treated sternly. Being docile and innocent, like you are, is not very common. The rest of us, me included, like you more because of that."

Her praise made me feel a strange sense of pride even as my body, tired as it was, began reacting to her touch, her words.

Amanda bit my earlobe gently as she continued to knead my breasts. "Your submission, excites us, makes us to want to do things to you. We are all taking advantage of you to act out some kinky fantasies with you, things we've always wanted to do to someone… I think I know the answer but …Do you like being tied up and ordered around?"

"…I never thought much about it… I kind of like it when my boyfriend is rough and just undresses me and takes me. I usually think about him holding me down and screwing me and that always get me off fast."

"I thought so… well! You're tired. I'll drive you home and you can think about how you feel about all of this."

"Amanda …it's kind of lonely at my place and I don't think I really want to go home." I whispered. I was afraid she'd make me leave.

Kate's Lesbian Awakening

"Ok. You can share my bed if you want to. Do you want to lie down and get some rest?"

"...What about the other girls?"

"How do you mean?"

"Well... they were gonna, you know, but you stopped them."

"Don't worry about them. They'll live."

"...but... they'll be disappointed..."

After a pause..."I guess I'm reading this wrong... you want to continue?"

"...I want them to like me." I admitted nervously.

"Oh! They like you all right... I don't know how long it will take before they're all done with "liking" you though? You might be here all night." She said coyly.

"...I don't mind." I whispered.

"Ok. I'll get them."

"...Amanda."

"Hmm?"

"...I liked... what you did before... to my hands." I admitted shyly.

Amanda just looked at me hard for a second, then turned me and retied my wrists with Stacy's pantyhose. This time they were in front of me, but I was still restrained.

"There you go Honey. Watch out for Stacy, she's got a real mean streak, yell out if she hurts you."

Amanda then helped me lay back down on the sofa. She put me on my back. Then she grabbed a cushion and put it under my hips. I felt so dirty laid out on the couch, completely nude, bound and on display. I felt my body tingling with anticipation as Amanda looked down at me. She stroked my cheek and I leaned into her hand. This seemed to please her. Then she gave me an almost chaste little kiss on the lips.

Amanda stood back up and looked down at me. She smiled and walked over to a small closet near the door. She opened it and reach inside. She pulled out a red silk scarf.

"Let's make this even more about feelings shall we?" She said and stepped over to me.

She took the scarf and tied it around my eyes.

"Might as well do it right, if you like being tied, you'll love being blindfolded. Everything OK?"

I nodded.

I could hear the girls come back in. They must have been just outside because they were all were back so quickly. I could also hear them giggling again.

In just a bit someone got on the couch above my head. Her knees were by my head and a wet open pussy settled down firmly on my mouth. With her fingers, she directed her large erect clit between my lips.

One of the girls, I think it was Pam, said "Just suck on this Honey, don't bother licking just suck it in hard, Oh yeah that's it, Suck."

I felt my legs being pulled apart and something was being rubbed against my soaking wet slit. I realized it was a dildo, though it felt different from the one they'd used before. Whatever the case, the up and down motion was driving me insane as I suckled on Pam's clit.

Whomever was holding the dildo knew what they were doing as they teased my lips and took the tip of the toy and circled my clit with it. I didn't think I could take much more of the teasing as I groaned into Pam's pussy. Then I felt the dildo stop sliding over my labia and it began to press into me. I was tight, but my pussy was so wet that it went in easily and penetrated deeply into my pussy. The cushion under my hips allowed the girl fucking me to reach further inside me than any real cock ever did and it felt heavenly.

As I experienced this strange new sense of fullness I continued sucking Pam's hard clit. She was so wet, her juices covered my face and as I worked her little love button with my lips she gripped my hair and mashed her hips down on my mouth and began groaning loudly as she came.

I felt her thigh muscles spasming with pleasure as she ground her body into my face.

I stopped sucking her clit and let my mouth open to taste more of her. Her fluids dripped into my hungry mouth, as she sat above me coming down. I felt my own orgasm build up and I started to scream into her cunt with pleasure as I came on the dildo that was slowly, deliciously, fucking me.

After the waves of pleasure passed, for both of us, Pam got off me. Only to be replaced by another girl almost immediately. The girl below me didn't stop fucking me just because I came. In fact her slow, steady strokes never stopped or even changed rhythm as I climaxed.

At first it was a little uncomfortable, my pussy had become so sensitive. But soon enough I got past that and began to rock my body in time with her motions. It was like my hips had a mind of their own as they rose up to meet her thrusts. I started crying out with pleasure when the girl above me said.

"Shut up and lick me slut." I felt her hips on my mouth and my tongue licked out and tasted her asshole. My nose was buried in her pussy. As I lapped at her and she wiggled her bum around on my face, laughing with pleasure.

"She's good! You like my little asshole don't you honey? Keep that sweet little tongue of yours moving baby. That's right stick it in there as deep as you can." She commanded as she groaned with pleasure and rode my face.

"That's right, French kiss my asshole you dirty little slut. You get it in there and do a good job now. Lick me nice and clean and I'll let you do that all the time."

I'd never had anyone talk to me that way before, it was so degrading... and so exciting. I wanted to do whatever I had to to please this woman. I could feel her moving as she masturbated herself furiously. She groaned out and almost crushed my face as she climaxed. The girl screwing me must have come at the same time. Both just fell on me resting and giggling.

Finally the warm bodies lifted off me. I heard them talking as the visiting girls Linda and Pam, said they had to leave. Melony said she was going off to bed. I heard them call, Good night to me, then doors opening and closing.

Kate's Lesbian Awakening

Amanda said. "Are you done with her?"

Stacy said, "No, I want to fool with her a while. Is that ok?"

"Yea. I guess. Don't hurt her, eh! She can sleep in my room when you're done."

"Don't worry about it, she'll be with me tonight. Go to sleep. Stop fussing, I won't hurt her."

"You still ok Honey?"

I nodded ok.

"Right, Good night then."

I heard her close her door and then Stacy's hands lightly ran over my body, at first gentle then she started lightly pinching my nipples.

It hurt but I didn't cry out.

"Come on lets have some serious fun with you. Get up."

Her hands assisted me to my feet and she held my shoulders and walked me into her bedroom. I heard her close and lock the door behind us. She sat me down her bed and I heard her looking for something in her dresser drawers. I heard her go into the bathroom and water was running.

When she came back Stacy untied my arms, removed my blindfold and led me to the hot tub she had poured for me. I was so confused I just let her treat me like a child as she gave me a long luxurious bath. Her soapy hands were all over my excited body even washing me in all secret places. She finished by shampooing my hair and rinsing me off. I was panting by the time she helped me out and dried me like a little girl. Wrapping my hair in a towel she led me back to the bed and placed me on top of the covers. She then turned off the light. I heard her undress and felt her warm naked body climb into bed beside me.

Stacy drew me in her arms and gave me a long passionate kiss that took my breath and senses away. She made love to me with skill and expertise. Finding pleasure centers on me that only a women could know about a female body. Her hands and lips brought me to climax after climax. It was all very fast and I was shocked by how my body was reacting. I'd had weekends where I'd had a lot of sex, but I'd had more orgasms in the past day than I had in the past month! It was almost too much for me to handle and it felt like every nerve in my body was tingling from stimulation.

I was perhaps most surprised when the beautiful blonde rolled me over on my stomach. She took one of the pillows from the bed and slid it under my hips. She never said anything while she worked my body and I just went along with her like the willing plaything that I was.

With my ass now propped up before her, Stacy gently spread my cheeks and her tongue touched my asshole. She showed that she had no reluctance in doing to me what she had made me to her. Her tongue probed and licked at all of my openings. Stacy's fingers gently brushed and caressed My body, reaching around me to touch my breasts even as her tongue savaged my ass.

I'd never had anyone do this to me. I honestly didn't think it would feel that good, I mean I'd had boyfriends who wanted to try anal and I'd let them. It was OK, but not that exciting. Having this luscious young woman explore my hole with her tongue as she expertly fingered my womanhood, it was a delight that quickly brought me to yet another shuddering orgasm.

As my body relaxed from the spasms of pleasure Stacy had induced, she moved away from me. I thought she might be done. She wasn't. She moved down to my feet and began massaging them. She spread my toes apart and expertly rubbed and squeezed my feet. It felt so good having her massaging me there that I didn't think it could get any better. Then I felt her tongue lick the bottom of my foot.

I jerked and let out a surprised squeal as her tongue played across the skin of the bottom of my foot. I wasn't normally ticklish, but this was almost torture. She didn't stop there though, now she stopped licking and began kissing then she sucked my toes. She took each of them into her mouth one at a time. She treated them like tiny cocks and gave each a quick little blow job. I thought I was going to scream from the way it overstimulated me, tickling me almost more than I could stand while at the same time making me want to cum again. It was all too much!

Finally she relented her oral assault on my feet and I relaxed again. She never asked, nor let me caress her.

"Just lie still." Was all she said to me as I tried to return the pleasure she was giving me.

Finally, after yet another shuddering climax I too was worn out and sore to take anymore.

"Please, no more." I asked in a husky whisper.

"Have you had enough pet?" She asked as she moved up to lay beside me on the bed.

Instead of answering her, I drew her to me and kissed her to gently. I could taste my own passion on her lips. She caressed my cheek and rolled over.

Very soon her breathing gentled as she fell into a deep sleep. As Stacy lay there next to me breathing in a steady, gentle rhythm. I was shocked as I realized that for the first time in my life someone had made love to me! She hadn't used me, she hadn't fucked me, she had made love to me!

I liked it and I liked Stacy. Hell I more than liked her. I realized I was, at that moment, in love with her.

That scarred me, but thinking about her excited me more than anything. I wanted to wake her and make love to her. I didn't though, after all the attention she'd paid to me I wanted to let her rest and not to disturb her.

I cuddled to her back and went to sleep inhaling her sweet personal essence.

-

Lips kissing my cheek woke me up. I opened my eyes to see Stacy already dressed standing by the bed. She smiled down at me.

"Good morning... little one... sleep well?" She asked.

I nodded and yawned, stretching my arms above my head.

"Let's get you up and some food in you. Do work or classes

today?"

"Sunday...No." I said, still working the sleepy fog of last night's pleasure from my brain.

"Take a shower, we're in the kitchen." She said as she opened the bedroom door and stepped into the hall.

When I came out showered and dressed. Amanda and Stacy were having coffee and one was poured for me.

Amanda smiled and asked. "Do you want some toast or cereal? We don't have any eggs or bacon, none of us like that stuff."

I told them no, the coffee was fine and then Amanda offered to give me a lift home but Stacy interrupted.

"No. I'll do it. We have to pick up her things. She's moving in my room with me for now for a week. Pat is planning on moving out in a week or so. She can stay with me until Melony's gone."

Both Amanda and I looked at her in surprise.

Stacy gave Amanda a wink and then they both turned and looked at me. Expectantly.

I was stunned. This was a decision that could affect my whole life and it was just thrown at me out of the blue. But what amazed me was the fact that I had already made up my mind. When she'd said that I was moving in with her it just felt... right. I'm not impulsive normally, but I just knew this was the right choice for me. I smiled and nodded in happiness.

Then Stacy looked at Amanda and said. "She's mine by the way! You may have found her, but she's mine. If you're good I'll let you borrow her sometimes."

They looked hard at each other but as their eyes turned towards me. I dropped mine and stared at my coffee, I couldn't tell if they were playing or what, but I didn't want to be in the middle of it. In fact, being treated somewhat like property was kind of exciting for me. It took a lot of worry from me to have them decide.

Amanda finally smiled and said "It's ok with me but give her a break eh! Have your fun but don't Fuck around with her feelings or you'll answer to me. I'm the one who brought her into our little arrangement and I don't want to see her hurt."

Stacy said nothing and Amanda stood up. She leaned over and gave me a kiss on the cheek.

"Welcome aboard Dear. Melony's off to Europe next week, some kind of semester abroad thing, but whatever the case, we've got lots of room... see you two later, I'm off for a jog."

She left the apartment leaving Stacy and I sitting alone.

Stacy said "Are you ready? I've just got a small car. Do we need a truck? I can borrow one if we do."

I told her no. I just had my clothes and my laptop, nothing that wouldn't go in a car.

As we left the apartment she locked the door and handed me a key. "This is my spare, yours, till we get you your own. You're living off campus right?"

I nodded.

"Ok, that's good. Dealing with the dorms at the college is such a hassle." She said as we entered the garage.

Her car was a late model sedan, a smaller but classy BMW, like my Dad always wanted but could never afford. After asking me where my place was. Stacy drove expertly through the light traffic till we were there.

My head was spinning and I was having second thoughts but as we entered my room I looked around at the shabby walls and remembered the nice apartment where I was moving into. Stacy helped, as I stood there looking around, not knowing where to start.

That's when I burst into tears.

"Oh goodness baby, what's wrong?" Stacy asked taking me into her arms.

I just cried into her shoulder and hugged her.

"Come on darling what is it?" She gently prodded.

I sniffled and pushed away from her, wiping my eyes. "I can't afford to move in with you. This place is a dump and I can barely afford it with tuition.

She took me back into her arms.

Kate's Lesbian Awakening

"Don't worry about money baby. Aside from the boat loads you'll make modeling with us, my family is kind of rich. I only live with Amanda and Melony because I like them. They're fun and when the mood hits their great playmates. So don't you worry about that. You'll be my guest until you start really earning some money modeling with us."

I sniffled and my tears dried up. Stacy pushed me back to look at my face and then she gently wiped my tears. "I'll make you happy hon. you'll do what I say, I'm bossy. But you'll be happy. OK?"

I nodded and smiled.

"Ok, where is your suitcase and we'll maybe need some garbage bags, let's see."

We spent the next couple of hours packing up my things and we must have made about a hundred trips down to her car. I started to wonder if it would all fit, but it did. I checked to see if we missed anything, but the room was clean. I didn't even take a last look around. Just locked the door and slipped the key back under it. Stacy said she'd message the landlord and take care of the lease and honestly, it didn't trouble me at all to leave that to her. If she was going to be bossy with me then she could take care of me too I decided.

When we got back to Stacy's car she asked me for my landlord's number. She called on her cell and handled the call like a professional. She told him I was distraught over a death in the family and would be leaving school.

I could hear him yelling at her over the phone about the lease and rent due. She just sat quietly listening to the tirade until he was done.

"If you're finished, I was about to say that I am a close family friend and I'll be handling the balance due on her lease. How much is it?" She asked, her voice calm and professional.

I couldn't hear the amount, but knew it was at least 3 months rent.

"Uh, huh... OK and how much do you have from the security deposit? Uh huh... OK. Can you accept credit card payments over the phone? OK, great." She said and then Stacy opened her purse and pulled out a small wallet. There must've been 20 credit cards in it when she opened it. She pulled out the first one, it was a platinum American Express card.

She read off the number and then had him read it back.

"OK so you'll charge the balance to that card and close the lease correct? Great. I'll see the charge on the card and I expect a receipt for that." She said and rattled off her... I mean our, apartment's address.

"You'll need to mail the deposit check to Kate also. You can make it out to her, but mail it to my address. Will that be a problem? OK, we'll go and confirm the apartment is vacant and collect the key, Kate slid it under the door. She won't be back." Stacy said and hung up on him.

Now I had to move...that bridge had been burned behind me I thought as we pulled out of the parking for my old place. We drove back to our place, I was amazed at how quickly that felt right to say. We pulled into the underground parking and started the process of unloading all of my stuff and taking it up to our place.

Stacy cleared out part of the closet and some dresser drawers for me and we put all my things away. After about an hour of going back and forth to the car, we both stopped and looked around, but there was nothing else to do. I was moved in.

Stacy smiled wickedly.

"You'd better not change your mind or you're doing THAT alone next time! Come on... lets have a shower."

She was undressing and was already in the shower under the hot water when I stepped in. Her body was small, but so toned and athletic. She didn't have an ounce of fat on her, but at the same time she was curvy and soft in all the right places. I was stunned by her beauty and it didn't take me long to become turned on as I looked at her cute little suds covered backside.

"Wash my back Kate," she said as she handed me the soap.

It was a command and I obeyed. I lathered up my hands and ran them over her shoulders and back. I was going over sections of her soft skin a second time when she said.

"Lower honey, do me all over." and spread her legs as she leaned over and pressed her hands on the wall. Her little ass stuck out towards me as I ran my soapy hands over her toned ass cheeks and then between her legs.

She groaned with pleasure. "Oh God Kate that feels good... I can't wait. Come on." She commanded and grabbed my hand and hauling me out of the shower and into the bedroom.

Her hands on my shoulders flipped me unto my back on the bed and fell forward onto me. She was on top of me and moved her body up until she was kneeling over my prone wet face. Her skin was glistening with wetness from the shower. Moisture dripped down on me off her body. Reaching down, her fingers spread her pussy open above me.

"Lick me quickly honey. Stick your fingers in my ass." She said huskily.

I immediately began to taste her womanhood even as my fingers found their way into her tight little ass. I gently probed into her, pushing until my finger entered her.

Stacy moaned with pleasure as my finger began to play gently in and out of her tight little asshole.

"Oh God yeah baby I like that. Oh yeah, that's right, just like that. Work your finger in deeper." She said as I brought another finger to gently wiggle its way in to join the first.

"Yes baby that's it! Now lick there." She groaned and her legs squeezed together around my head.

"That's it Kate, now lick me faster come on faster."

I did as I was told and worked my tongue up and down her wet labia as fast as I could. She pressed her body down onto my face and my tongue lapped inside her folds furiously as my soapy fingers played in and out of her ass.

Stacy ground her wet pussy unto my face and humped my mouth as she came. Her legs squeezed me even tighter as her body shook with waves of pleasure. I was so happy to bring her this much joy. She'd pleased me so much last night I loved having the chance to return the favor.

I kept working her cunt even as the orgasm faded and then she let out a squeal of delight and came again in a shocking, fast, hard, follow-up. For a second I thought she might crush my skull her legs were clamping onto me so tightly, but then the wave of pleasure past and she fell forward onto the bed above me.

Somehow my fingers had managed to stay inside her ass and I started to withdraw them, but her hand reached down and held them in her as she lay beside me recovering. With her legs still wrapped around my head, she reached down and pulled my hands away from her, my fingers sliding out of her tight opening.

Taking hold of my hand she directed my just probing fingers to my lips.

"Suck them, go on.... clean them." She shoved them in my mouth and looked at me with a mischievous grin. I gingerly sucked on my fingers, which had just been buried deep in her ass. I could taste her womanly juices, and something else, it wasn't unpleasant, but it was different. It felt somehow more intimate to me than just tasting her pussy juices. This was something taboo. Something forbidden. That made it exciting.

"Are they clean?"

I nodded yes.

"Good girl. We going to have a great time together and I'm sure going to enjoy training you." She purred and pulled herself off of me.

She got up and offered me her hand. "Let's get dressed and brush your teeth. While you do that, I'll see what we have around for lunch."

I smiled and went to the bathroom. My toothbrush was still in my little overnight bag and I fished it out and began to brush just as she'd told me to. I liked being told what to do.

As I cleaned my teeth it occurred to me that I was going to have to tell my parent soon. What would I tell them? I worried about that for a moment and then decided to just tell them that I'd found some new roommates and moved into a better place. My love life was none of their business after all.

Then it occurred to me that I'd have to tell my boyfriend something too... or would I? Maybe I would just let him wonder for a while. That wouldn't be nice, but then again now that I'd had someone really please me, I realized just how little he'd cared for my needs. So I definitely didn't feel bad for him.

All these thoughts ran through me as I brushed my teeth and by the time I was done with them, I felt like I was at peace with myself and the situation. So I slipped into the bedroom, our bedroom, I amended mentally, and put on my clothes.

When I joined her in the kitchen Stacy had made us up sandwiches and a pot of tea. We sat eating and chatting. She asked me about myself and in a while she knew pretty well, all there was to tell. She asked if my boyfriend was going to mind the new arrangements we'd just made and I shrugged.

"I'm not so sure he's still relevant to me at this point." I said and Stacy smiled.

"You seem to have taken to all these changes rather well." She said.

"It's not the changes I've taken to, it's the way you treat me. It shows me just how little he really cared for my needs." I admitted.

Stacy didn't say anything, she just nodded and sipped her tea.

I asked Stacy how much I would need to pay as my share of the apartment rental. She didn't answer.

"Look Stacy, you just paid off my lease, I want to start contributing as soon as I can." I said and she looked at me for a long moment.

"You have a part time job while you're in school right?" She asked.

I nodded.

"So how much are you making there:"

When I told her she smiled.

"You liked modeling. I think we will just get you more work doing that. It will give you a lot more time to enjoy life and for school and you'll also make much more money." She said.

"In addition to doing more modeling I can also give you some other little assignments." She continued.

"I like the modeling idea but I'm not sure what you mean by 'other assignments'". I admitted shyly.

She smiled that mischievous grin again and promised I wouldn't be doing nothing I didn't like or want to do. She left it at that as Amanda came back from jogging. She joined us and we briefly talked about how the move went. Stacy said to Amanda that we had to find more modeling assignments for me.

Amanda gave me a sly smile and said "More competition eh! Well you can work with me anytime Love," and gave me a peck on the cheek.

She went off to take a shower and I saw Stacy watching her as she left. We sat drinking our teas and after a while Stacy came over to me and gave me a kiss. We heard the water in the shower turn off and Stacy smiled.

"Honey Amanda just finished her shower. Go in to her room and tell her I sent you."

At my puzzled look Stacy said. "Go on Honey. You like Amanda don't you? It's no big deal just make her feel good, like you did me. Off you go now."

As I walked down the hallway towards Amanda's room. I realized I was on my first "assignment".

END

www.ingramcontent.com/pod-product-compliance
Lightning Source LLC
Chambersburg PA
CBHW051501140726
47987CB00006B/2830